# Sammy

by May Justus

© 2019 Jenny Phillips

goodandbeautiful.com

Cover design by Elle Staples

Cover illustration by
Embla Granqvist and Christine Chisholm

ACKNOWLEDGMENT

*The author wishes to thank
Mr. Mellinger E. Henry
for his version of the folk song
used in this book.*

Illustrated by Christine Chisholm

Originally published in 1946

The Pennybacker's cabin

Mammy Pennybacker and Sammy

Pappy Pennybacker

## THERE WAS A LITTLE TREE

# Sammy

The Pennybackers were planting corn in the patch below their cabin.

Pappy Pennybacker was behind his plow, laying off the rows.

Mammy Pennybacker was dropping in the kernels, four at a time.

Sammy followed his mother, covering the shining kernels with his hoe.

But Sammy's mind wasn't on his work. He was thinking about something far away from this corn patch—about three things, to tell the truth.

The first thing was a pair of new shoes that cost two dollars.

The second thing was a pair of new blue britches that cost one dollar.

The third thing was a blue-and-white striped shirt that cost one dollar.

Four dollars in all. Sammy sighed deeply. He had seen all three of these things last Saturday in a big store at Far Beyant. Far Beyant was five miles away on Yon Side of the mountain. He and Pappy sold wood and kindling there sometimes, when they were lucky. Then they brought home flour for biscuit bread, a small sack of sugar (so they could have pie for a treat on Sunday), a box of soda, or a poke of salt.

There was never money for new clothes till berry-picking time in the summer. Again Sammy sighed. If only he could have fine new clothes for the Last Day of School. Folks came from near and far for the program on Last Day. All the children had pieces to speak and songs to sing. It was going to be a wonderful occasion.

This year Sammy had something special to do on the program—a song to sing while he played his banjo. It was a funny old song all right. He had picked it up, little by little, by hearing folks sing one verse of it at a time. Now he had learned it all by heart, and he was going to surprise everyone.

Thinking of that surprise, Sammy chuckled to himself. Then the smile left his face. He'd look like a scarecrow, like as not. Even his best shirt and britches were so patched up they looked like a crazy quilt.

As for shoes, he had none—none at all. They had worn out with the winter. He had turned barefoot a month ago while the frost still nipped his toes. He didn't mind so mighty much for himself, that is. He was used to the feel of going barefoot most of the year. But the looks of it—that was a different thing. There

wasn't one of the other children who would be barefoot on the Last Day of School.

If only Pappy and Mammy had money enough to send to the mail order house! Some of the boys and girls had already ordered brand new clothes out of the wish book. Packages from the mail order company had already come.

This minute a wish book was lying on the shelf in the Pennybacker's cabin. In it there were

This minute a wish book was lying on the shelf

pictures of fine shoes and shirts and britches like those Sammy wanted. He had looked at those pages so often he knew just how much the clothes he wanted would cost. But he had said nothing to Pappy and Mammy. He would just have to go without until berry-picking time.

Well, he'd better be paying attention to this job he was doing. Corn planting was particular work. He couldn't do it any old how.

He was glad that this was yellow corn they were planting. It showed up plainer than the white corn in the rooty, rocky rows of their new field which had been cleared last winter.

Cling—clang, cling—clang! went Sammy's hoe as it struck against the stones, making a sort of music to the old planting rhyme that was running through his head. As he went on covering the corn, he began to hum the song to the cling-clang music which his hoe made:

Cling–clang, cling–clang! went Sammy's hoe

"One for the cutworm,
One for the crow,
One for the field mouse,
One to grow."

This meant that four grains of corn should be planted to a hill. Sammy always counted out four grains before covering them up.

All of a sudden, he looked up and saw that Pappy and Mammy had stopped at the edge of the field to rest and get a drink out of the water jug which had been cooling in the shade of a big oak tree.

Sammy hurried to finish his row and catch up with them. He was hot and tired and thirsty. The jug looked inviting.

Cling—clang went his hoe as he swung it faster and faster.

"One - two - three - four." He counted out the grains of corn as he plodded along. He was so

Pappy and Mammy had stopped to get a drink

intent on his work that he didn't see what Pappy and Mammy saw—a man riding in the Hollow. About a half minute later, he heard Pappy yell, "It's Brother Sam!"

When he heard that, Sammy dropped his hoe in a hurry.

By the time it had hit the ground, he had reached the end of his row. From the place where Pappy and Mammy stood, there was a little clearing through which a trail wound up the Hollow. Yes, a man on a mule was riding up the trail.

Sammy looked at him closely, tossing his dark-colored forelock back and squinting his eyes against the sun. He caught his breath in a sighful manner. "It's Rowdy, Uncle Sam's mule. But the man isn't Uncle Sam!"

There was a moment's silence then, as Pappy and Mammy and Sammy stared with keen eyes down the Hollow trail.

Yes, a man on a mule was riding up the trail

"Look in my saddlebag!" Uncle Sam would cry

"Bats and bullfrogs!" Pappy muttered. "The boy's right about it. Somebody else is riding Brother Sam's mule."

"Mercy on us!" Mammy sighed. "I hope it means no trouble has happened to any of the kinfolks on Yon Side."

"Amen!" Pappy went on in a sober-some voice. Pappy spoke as if he were in the meetinghouse, agreeing to something the Circuit Rider had to say.

Sammy said nothing. He couldn't speak for the mully-grubby feeling that filled his heart that moment with disappointment. Whenever Uncle Sam came from Yon Side, he always brought a present to Sammy, who was his namesake.

"Look in my saddlebag!" he would cry as soon as he had howdied everyone with a handshake. "Look in my saddlebag!"

Sammy was never slow to do as he was bidden. For there was always something new in the saddlebag. A gift for him—a namesake gift, as Uncle Sam called it. Sometimes there were gifts for Pappy and Mammy as well.

The boy smiled as he remembered certain of the treasures which Uncle Sam had given him—a popgun fashioned from a hollow cane, a top whittled from a pine knot, a good quill whistle, and a pair of mittens made out of rabbit skin. Yes, he was always glad to see Uncle Sam coming, riding his mule Rowdy.

Yet who was this strange man riding Rowdy up the trail?

The stranger rode up near the fence

"Bats and bullfrogs!" Pappy cried again. "He looks like an outlander man. He's got on a store-boughten suit of clothes, sure as shootin'. A new-fangled hat, too, I vow and declare. Yep, he's an outlander man!"

"Do tell," Mammy murmured in wonderment. "Maybe it's a new Circuit Rider. Or maybe," she added, "it's a peddler man!"

Sammy said nothing because he had no answer to the riddle.

The stranger rode up near the fence and smiled in a friendly fashion. He howdied the Pennybackers, and they howdied him.

"Is your name Tom Pennybacker?" asked the stranger.

"Reckon so," replied Pappy in a cautious way.

"Mine's Dave Hunter," the stranger said. "I spent last night with your brother on Yon Side. He lent me his mule to ride over here today."

Pappy nodded.

The stranger went on: "They call me Mr. Songcatcher. I'm making a search in these mountains for old songs. I want to put them in a book, so they will not be forgotten."

Again Pappy nodded, and Mr. Songcatcher continued once more: "Some of these songs are so old, they were brought from England and Scotland by the people who came to these mountains and settled here long ago. The songs are called ballads. And I have written down a good many of them—*Lady Alice, Barbara Allen, Tom Bolyn, The Golden Vanity*, and several others."

Mr. Songcatcher paused.

Pappy Pennybacker nodded a third time, and in a much friendlier way. "Good old songs, good old songs, all of 'em," Pappy said. "Good songs to sing, and mighty fine tunes to play, too," he added.

Mammy's face was friendlier too beneath her old bonnet.

Sammy listened with both ears.

From his seat on Rowdy's back, the outlander went on: "Just now, I'm on the lookout for a certain song I've heard about. I know a little of it, but that is all. Some of the people I've asked about it say it's only a fiddle jig. Others call it a banjo tune. But it's a song, I'm sure, for it starts out like a story.

"Your brother thought perhaps you knew it. Listen! The tune of it goes like this—" and the outlander started to whistle. Then he stopped and sang what he knew of the song:

>"There was a little tree,
>
>The prettiest little tree,
>
>The sweetest little tree
>
>You ever did see—"

"That's all I know, but there is more to it. Your brother Sam remembered that this song tells about a bird and a nest in the tree. He couldn't think just how it goes."

Mr. Songcatcher looked straight at Sammy

Then the outlander turned right to Pappy and said, "When your brother told me what a fine ballad singer you used to be, I came right over!"

"That tune sounds familiar-like," Pappy agreed, "but the song's leaked out of my head."

Sammy drew a deep breath. His face was fairly shining with the gladsome feeling inside him. He couldn't speak to save himself, not before this stranger man, this outlander. But oh, what a fine secret he had all to himself.

For Sammy knew that tune! Besides, he knew every word in it. *There Was a Little Tree*—it was his surprise piece for the Last Day of School.

All of a sudden, without meaning to, he started to hum the tune. At the sound, Mr. Songcatcher turned from Pappy and looked straight at Sammy.

"You must have heard that song before to carry the tune so well!"

Sammy swallowed so hard, he nearly choked. He felt as scared as a rabbit when a body slips up on him from behind a stump. All eyes were on Sammy now.

Pappy chuckled. "Sing the song if you know it, Sammy, and help Mr. Songcatcher out."

"Yes," said Mammy, "go ahead, Sammy. Speak when you're spoken to in a mannerly way."

Now Mr. Songcatcher was smiling at Sammy, but the boy looked the other way.

"Reckon he's bashful," Pappy said.

"It looks," declared Mammy, "as if the old cat's got his tongue."

Sammy wiggled his toes in the dirt, his eyes on the ground. He had never felt so scared in his life. He wanted to sing the song. He wanted to very much, but he couldn't seem to get started.

He turned in his tracks and ran off along the trail toward the door of the Pennybacker cabin.

He turned in his tracks and ran toward the cabin

When he got to the cabin, he ran inside to his banjo

Behind him he could hear them all calling—
Pappy, Mammy, and the outlander man. But
Sammy ran on and on. If he could carry out
his notion—

When he got to the cabin, he ran inside and
across the room to the wall where his banjo
was hanging. Taking the banjo down gently, he
strummed the strings and smiled to himself. For
he had decided that it wouldn't scare him to sing
that song before a stranger if he had his banjo to
help him carry the tune. Yes, this was his notion.

Tucking the banjo under his arm, he started
back. Pappy and Mammy were once more
busy with their corn planting. Mr. Songcatcher
was sitting alone on the old rail fence, with
Rowdy cropping the grass behind him. When
Sammy came up, the outlander never said a
word. But he smiled at Sammy. Sammy knew
then that Mr. Songcatcher understood. He

understood that Sammy was shy but not lacking in manners.

The boy smiled back. He didn't feel a bit afraid anymore. He would do his very best to sing and play the song for the outlander.

*Twang—twang*! Sammy's fingers plucked the strings of his banjo, found the right notes, and went on—*tum-tum-tum*! Then he opened his mouth and started to sing. He knew that he must keep going right through all the verses and not get out of breath.

At the first twang, Mr. Songcatcher took a notebook and pencil out of his pocket. When Sammy began to sing, Mr. Songcatcher began to write down the words:

> "There was a little tree,
> The prettiest little tree,
> The sweetest little tree
> You ever did see.

Mr. Songcatcher was sitting alone on the old rail fence

> The tree in the ground,
>
> And the green grass growing
>
> All around, all around,
>
> And the green grass growing
>
> All around!"

"That's it, that's it!" cried Mr. Songcatcher eagerly. "Sing on, Sonny! Sing on. Don't stop. I will pay you for every verse as you go along." He laughed out loud in excitement. Reaching into his pocket, he laid a piece of money on the top rail of the fence. A twenty-five cent piece it was. A quarter of a dollar.

"Whoo-pee, hoo-ray!" thought Sammy to himself as he started the next verse:

> "There was a little limb,
>
> The prettiest little limb,
>
> The sweetest little limb
>
> You ever did see.
>
> The limb in the tree,

"There was a little tree, the prettiest little tree"

> The tree in the ground,
>
> And the green grass growing
>
> All around, all around,
>
> And the green grass growing
>
> All around!"

Sammy stopped to get a good breath.

Mr. Songcatcher nodded. "I've got all that down. Sing on." He laid another quarter on the fence rail alongside of the first coin.

"I'm making money in a hip-and-hurry," Sammy thought to himself. Then he took

another good breath and went on playing and singing:

> "There was a little branch,
> The prettiest little branch,
> The sweetest little branch
> You ever did see.
> The branch in the limb,
> The limb in the tree,
> The tree in the ground,
> And the green grass growing
> All around, all around,
> And the green grass growing
> All around!"

Mr. Songcatcher smiled. "Go ahead, don't stop now!" he cried and laid a third quarter on the fence rail.

A *twang-twang* came from Sammy's banjo, and the boy went on:

"There was a little twig,

The prettiest little twig,

The sweetest little twig

You ever did see.

The twig in the branch,

The branch in the limb,

The limb in the tree,

The tree in the ground,

And the green grass growing

All around, all around,

And the green grass growing

All around!"

This time Mr. Songcatcher didn't speak. He just slid another quarter along the fence rail, and Sammy sang on.

"There was a little leaf,

The prettiest little leaf,

The sweetest little leaf

You ever did see.

The leaf in the twig,

The twig in the branch,

The branch in the limb,

The limb in the tree,

The tree in the ground,

And the green grass growing

All around, all around,

And the green grass growing

All around!"

Sammy stopped. He had seen Mr. Songcatcher's hand go into his pocket again. How much money did the outlander have? There were a lot more verses to come. "This is a pretty lengthy song," Sammy said slowly.

"That's all right, Sammy," Mr. Songcatcher laughed back. "My bargain holds because this song is worth a great deal to me. In fact, I'm wondering what is coming next."

Sammy felt right happy to hear the outlander man say that. He grinned at Pappy and Mammy, who had stopped their work and had come close to listen.

"There was a little nest,
The prettiest little nest,
The sweetest little nest
You ever did see.
The nest in the leaf,
The leaf in the twig,
The twig in the branch,
The branch in the limb,
The limb in the tree,
The tree in the ground,
And the green grass growing

All around, all around,

And the green grass growing

All around!"

"I bet I know what's coming next," Mr. Songcatcher chuckled. "Eggs for the nest!"

Sammy smiled. "I reckon you're right," he said. But before he went on singing, he did some quick figuring in his head. One, two, three, four, five, six quarters on the fence. That made a dollar and a half.

With the verse and one more after that, he'd have two dollars. This was enough to buy that pair of shoes in the Far Beyant store—new shoes for the Last Day of School!

Just then the boy heard Pappy Pennybacker calling to him: "Sonny, you'd better get your hoe and cover the last hills of corn. If you don't, the crows'll get it while we're gone to dinner."

"Give me a hoe, too, and I'll help you," Mr. Songcatcher said then.

Sammy hung his banjo on a tree and, feeling carefully inside his pocket to make sure there was no hole, dropped in the six quarters.

"I could sing the rest of the song to you while we work," he told Mr. Songcatcher, as he handed the outlander the hoe.

"Fine!" said Mr. Songcatcher. "You start, and I'll sing it with you. That will help me to remember it till I can write it down."

"Give me a hoe too, and I'll help you"

Sammy hung his banjo on a tree

As they finished covering the corn, Sammy and Mr. Songcatcher sang the rest of the funny old song:

> "There was a little egg,
> 
> The prettiest little egg,
> 
> The sweetest little egg
> 
> You ever did see.
> 
> The egg in the nest,
> 
> The nest in the leaf,
> 
> The leaf in the twig,
> 
> The twig in the branch,
> 
> The branch in the limb,
> 
> The limb in the tree,
> 
> The tree in the ground,
> 
> And the green grass growing
> 
> All around, all around,
> 
> And the green grass growing
> 
> All around!

"There was a little bird,

The prettiest little bird,

The sweetest little bird

You ever did see.

The bird in the egg,

The egg in the nest,

The nest in the leaf,

The leaf in the twig,

The twig in the branch,

The branch in the limb,

The limb in the tree,

The tree in the ground,

And the green grass growing

As they finished covering the corn, they sang the rest of the song

"It's nigh about dinner time by the sunball"

All around, all around,

And the green grass growing

All around!"

Chink! Chink! Mr. Songcatcher dropped two more quarters into Sammy's pocket.

"Mighty much obliged to you," Sammy replied happily. He would have those new shoes, certain sure! No doubt about it now.

But Mr. Songcatcher was speaking. "Oh no, it is I who am very much obliged to you," he said.

He would have said more, but by this time Pappy Pennybacker was calling again: "It's nigh about dinner time by the sunball. Let's all hurry up!"

In no time at all, the Pennybackers and their visitor were sitting around the table in the cabin kitchen. The dinner had been kept hot in the big black pot on the chimney hook and in the oven on the hearth. There was thick stirabout soup, corn pone brown and crusty to eat, and big cups of spicy sassafras tea to drink.

"Not much of a company meal," Mammy Pennybacker kept saying. "But there's a-plenty of it, such as it is."

"A better meal I never ate," declared Mr. Songcatcher. "All in all, I consider this one of my luckiest days!"

"A lucky day for me, too." Sammy spoke up from his end of the table. Then he took the

In no time at all, they were sitting around the table

money from his pocket and laid the pieces in a row. "Eight quarters—two dollars in all!" he cried proudly. "Mr. Songcatcher paid me that for singing that ballad song."

"Praise Him above!" Mammy cried from one side of the table.

"Bats and bullfrogs!" yelled Pappy from the other side of the table.

"And what are you going to buy with your riches?" Mr. Songcatcher asked.

"Buy new shoes," Sammy promptly told him. "New shoes to wear on the Last Day of School, when I stand up to play my piece."

"But you need a new shirt more than you do shoes," Mammy declared.

"And new britches," said Pappy. "You've no call for shoes this time of year."

Sammy's mouth trembled as he tried to speak. He did want those new shoes so very much. "I'd rather wear raggedy clothes and have new shoes," he said at last. "Besides, two dollars won't buy new shoes and a new shirt and new britches. Two dollars is only exactly enough for new shoes from the store in Far Beyant."

Pappy Pennybacker looked at Sammy for a minute without saying anything. Then he grunted, "All right. All right."

"All right," echoed Mammy in a sighful way.

Mr. Songcatcher said nothing at all. He just went on looking out the open window at the crooked mountain trail that twisted and turned till it disappeared down the Hollow.

"Well," said Pappy Pennybacker, getting up, "it's time to go back to work."

"And it's time for me to be on my way," Mr. Songcatcher told them.

He shook hands with Pappy and Mammy and Sammy and thanked them for his dinner,

Sammy brought Rowdy to the front yard gate

promising to come back as soon as he could, certain-sure.

Then he said, "Bring around the mule, Sonny."

Sammy brought Rowdy to the front yard gate. Mr. Songcatcher stood close beside Sammy as he put his hand on his shoulder and said, "Good luck to you, boy."

Then he swung into the saddle, turning around to the boy to say, "And I think you're going to have some good luck mighty soon, Sammy. In fact, I wouldn't be surprised if it came along today. When it does, just remember that you helped me find something I needed very badly. Your song is going to be one of the best songs in my book. Perhaps it will even be the very best."

Sammy smiled at that and answered, "I'm glad, Mr. Songcatcher. Thank you, and come again."

He waved to Mr. Songcatcher until the outlander had disappeared from sight around the bending trail.

As Sammy turned back toward the cabin, he slid his hand down into his pocket. He wanted to hear those quarters jingle. But his fingers went down into something soft, not into the hard quarters. His heart pounded. Had he lost his money already? Jerking his hand from his pocket, the soft something tightly held between his fingers, Sammy looked down.

Two one-dollar bills! So this was the good luck Mr. Songcatcher had been talking about. The outlander must have slipped the money into the pocket when he was standing close beside Sammy.

The boy's eyes blinked in surprise. All of a sudden—whoopee, hurrah! Four dollars in all! He saw himself on the Last Day of School—up

Had he lost his money already?

in front, all fancy fine in his new shoes, a new shirt, and new blue britches, with his banjo under his arm. He was starting to sing his funny old song—"*There was a little tree, the prettiest little tree—*"

He stopped abruptly and shouted, "Pappy! Mammy!" and ran off toward the corn patch, lickety-split.

He ran off toward the corn patch, lickety-split

# More Books from The Good and the Beautiful Library!

## Beanie Boxed Set
by Ruth Latrobe Carroll

Beanie Tatum has a heart full of adventure and a desire for companionship. When Beanie forms an unbreakable bond with his dog, Tough Enough, and his pony, Sassy, he sets out to prove that Sassy and Tough Enough are more than just animals; they're part of the family. Readers will love the joy and adventures they experience as they explore the Tatum's farm in the Great Smoky Mountains and witness the growth of a friendship that cannot be forgotten.

## The Journey of Ching Lai
by Eleanor Frances Lattimore

One beautiful day, Ching Lai and his cousin are surprised to find a riderless black donkey coming down the path. Trying to look courageous to his cousin, Ching Lai climbs on the donkey's back. When the donkey starts to trot away, Ching Lai does not dare get off. Ching Lai soon finds himself far away from his mountain home and caught in a journey that takes him farther and farther away.

GOODANDBEAUTIFUL.COM